"*Montana Cherries* is a heartwarming yet heart-wrenching story of the heroine's struggle to accept the truth about her mother's death—and life."

—*RT Book Reviews*, 4 stars

"An entertaining romance with a well-developed plot and believable characters. The chemistry between Vega and JP is explosive and will have you rooting for the couple's success. Readers will definitely look forward to more works by this author."

—*RT Book Reviews*, 4 stars on Caught on Camera

"Kim Law pens a sexy, fast-paced romance."

—*New York Times* bestselling author Lori Wilde on *Caught on Camera*

"A solid combination of sexy fun."

—*New York Times* bestselling author Carly Phillips on *Ex on the Beach*

"*Sugar Springs* is a deeply emotional story about family ties and second chances. If you love heartwarming small towns, this is one place you'll definitely want to visit."

"Filled with engaging characters, *Sugar Springs* is the typical everyone-knows-everyone's-business small town. Law skillfully portrays heroine Lee Ann's doubts and fears, as well as hero Cody's struggle to be a better person than he believes he can be. And Lee Ann's young nieces are a delight."

Montana
INSPIRED

ALSO BY KIM LAW

The Wildes of Birch Bay

Montana Inspired (prequel)

Montana Cherries

Montana Rescue

Montana Mornings

Montana Mistletoe

Montana Dreams

Montana Promises

Montana Homecoming

Montana Ever After

Sugar Springs Novels

Sugar Springs

Sweet Nothings

Sprinkles on Top

Turtle Island Novels

Ex on the Beach

Hot Buttered Yum Two

Turtle Island Doves (novella)

On the Rocks

Montana
INSPIRED

Kim Law

J-KO PUBLISHING

Copyright © 2021 by Kim Law
Published by J-Ko Publishing
Cover Design Copyright © 2021 The Killion Group, Inc

ISBN: 978-1-950908-18-9

CHAPTER ONE

H*oly hotness.*

Jewel Jackson licked the cherry-flavored ice cream of the two-scoop cone she'd just been handed as her attention snagged on the man manning the booth opposite where she stood. Bobby Brandon was home again. Which she'd *known*. Or she'd known he *would* be home. As he'd done the year before, after his father had died, Bobby intended to help out with his family's stock contracting business. Jewel's full-time hand was on leave for the next month, so Bobby had offered to fill the void.

But Bobby Brandon, back in town so soon after the last time . . . *and* with a full, thick beard? Not to mention, the wildly inviting messy hair pushed back from his face.

Good Lord.

It hadn't even been seven months since she'd seen the man. Why the big change?

And who knew she liked bearded men?

She scooped out another bite of ice cream with her tongue,

taking a moment to enjoy the sweetness of the locally grown cherries before swallowing. She'd always been more drawn to a clean-shaven face, such as what Montana's bull riders typically sported. A few of the guys maintained trim goatees, but in her neck of the woods, most of the cowboys were fresh-faced and whip-cord tough.

Bobby was . . .

Sigh.

Bobby was the friend she'd always quietly lusted after while also knowing she could never have. He'd been hot before. A little beefier than the bull riders. A lot nerdier. And clean-shaven with short, neat hair.

He'd also always been taken. He had Bria.

He'd *always* had Bria.

And they had big plans.

Yet now, there was a sexy, just-say-the-word-and-I'll-back-you-against-a wall look about him as his blue eyes seemed to twinkle from the middle of all that hair, and Jewel found that she couldn't drag her gaze away from him.

He hadn't seen her yet. He remained focused on the mother and son who stood in front of him. They were at Birch Bay's annual cherry festival, and as Bobby had done occasionally over the years, he'd rented a booth to sell his wood carvings. He'd dabbled in the hobby for as long as Jewel had known him, even gifting her a tiny bull after she'd started working for his dad back in high school.

The pieces had an unpolished roughness about them, but at the same time were exquisite. The curves weren't smoothed out. Instead, everything he made showcased the small slivers shaved off to form each shape. However, the added details were phenomenal. He mostly did animals, but she'd seen

2

holiday themed items, as well. Santa Clauses and snowmen. Cupids and leprechauns. That sort of thing. His pieces had been in one of the local tourist shops for the last couple of years, and Jewel found his creativity humbling.

"When are you going to stop ogling from afar and simply go for it?"

The unexpected question had her entire body jerking in surprise, her gaze shooting from Bobby to the man now standing at her side, and as the top scoop of her ice cream wobbled precariously, her free hand barely made it up in time to catch it.

"*Nick Wilde*," she hissed. She held the cold pink blob in her right hand and did her best to reattach it to the cone. "I am *not* ogling. I was just admiring Bobby's carvings."

His laugh was half snort. "Well, you were certainly admiring *something*."

She scowled, but he didn't notice because he'd reached over to the booth where she'd bought the ice cream and snatched up a handful of napkins. The booth was a miniature version of his family's local store, The Cherry Basket, which was a side business to their cherry orchard. The Wildes had one of the largest operations on the eastern shore of Montana's Flathead Lake, and though several of the Wildes no longer lived in Birch Bay, most usually returned for the annual harvest and subsequent cherry festival. Nick was one of those who regularly returned.

He wiped her hand off when she thrust it out for him, and though she wanted to further defend herself against "ogling" Bobby, she used the excuse of her now very unstable ice cream cone as a detractor.

Focusing on smoothing out the scoops, as well as catching

3

every dribble oozing over the edges of the cone, she made sure her gaze stayed trained *only* on her ice cream.

"Admit it, J," Nick murmured as he leaned in to whisper in her ear. "You've had the hots for Bobby since he was a mere boy."

"*Shhh.*" She glared at him. "And *no*. I haven't."

She moved away from the booth, as well as the clump of other customers standing nearby. The streets were packed today since it was a perfect seventy-six-degree July day. Residents of Birch Bay, as well as tourists from all over, looked forward to this festival every year.

Nick gave her a bored look as he shifted to remain standing next to her. He was one of those cowboys she'd just been thinking about. There was a good chance he'd top the list in the Montana Pro this year, especially if he finished the season the way he'd started it. However, he *wasn't* a cowboy she'd ever lusted after. They'd been friends since the fourth grade.

"I hear he's come home to help *you* for the next few weeks," Nick prodded.

The fast spread of information in her hometown never failed. "He's home to help out in his *family's* business."

"By traveling to the rodeos with *you*."

She once again glared at him. "Yes . . . *So?*" It wasn't best practice to handle the bulls solo at the rodeos, and she couldn't bring either of her other two employees due to them needing to stay back and care for the rest of the stock. Therefore, yes, Bobby would be traveling with her for the next five weekends as a second set of hands.

"*So*," Nick stressed. "I'm just saying that maybe it's time you finally go for it."

"There's nothing to go for, even if I wanted to. He's engaged to Bria." She bit down into her ice cream.

"That's not what I hear. Crawley's brother dates Bria's sister."

Jewel couldn't help herself. She peeked over at Nick as he continued talking. Bria's sister *did* date James Crawley, one of the other guys on the circuit.

"Word is that lover boy over there and Bria broke up over a month ago. For *good* this time."

Jewel made a face. Bobby and Bria never broke up for good. "I'll believe it when I see it." He would likely head straight back to her the minute he finished up here—if not before. Bobby and Bria Riggs had dated on and off since freshman year of high school, all the way through college, and had gotten engaged sometime in the last couple of years. It was unclear if the engagement had happened before graduation or after, but nonetheless, "they" weren't going anywhere.

Bobby would return to Missoula next month to start school for his pharmacy degree—he'd delayed beginning the year before due to staying in Birch Bay after his father died—then the two of them would eventually walk down the aisle, buy the perfect house, pop out a few kids, and live happily ever after. It was the plan, after all. Which made it a good thing *she* wasn't interested.

Nick shook his head. "It's different this time. He's the one who broke up with her." He nodded toward Bobby. "Plus, look at him. *He's* different. Something has definitely changed. I think Crawley might be right."

She did look at Bobby then. And what she saw set her pulse pounding.

The mother and son had left, presumably with their

purchases, and now Ashlee Anderson stood at his booth. Ashlee was leaning in, a hefty dose of cleavage showing, a smile a mile wide, and Bobby looked more than interested.

He leaned her way, as well.

His mouth curved naughtily in the middle of all that facial hair.

And his eyes couldn't seem to keep from straying to her chest.

"For the love of . . ."

She let her words trail off, and Nick laughed again.

Nick nudged. "You going to sit back and let another girl swoop in after all this time?"

"He's just a friend," she reminded him. But even to her own ears, she knew the proclamation sounded weak. The fact was, though, that Bobby *had* always been just a friend. Or more like a big brother.

She'd worked for his dad for the last seven years, since the day she'd turned sixteen, and had volunteered out at the ranch even before then. Due to Blake Brandon's unexpected death, she'd been promoted to manager of Double B Pro Rodeo, and throughout it all, Bobby had never shown even the slightest hint of interest.

Still . . . she wasn't about to sit by and watch him make a stupid mistake with Ashlee. That girl would chew him up and spit him out in a single bite. While *smiling* the entire time.

Tossing the remainder of her uneaten cone in the nearest trash can, she pumped a squirt of waterless soap into her palm from the hand-cleaning station, and after removing any lingering stickiness, wiped her hands down the sides of her jeans. She then reset her sights on the opposite side of the road.

"Interested or not," she mumbled, "I won't stand back and watch him get mixed up with the likes of her."

CHAPTER TWO

Bobby kept his eyes trained on Ashlee even as he sensed Jewel nearing. He'd caught sight of her standing on the other side of the street earlier, and he'd wanted to wave her over. He hadn't managed to catch up with her since arriving back in town yet. But then Nick Wilde had shown up, and something unexpected spurred to life. Something that had caught him completely off guard.

Jealousy.

For *Jewel*.

He had zero reason to be jealous of Jewel Jackson talking to another man. But the feeling was even more illogical given the man in question was Nick.

She and Nick had been thick as thieves ever since elementary school. But more importantly, *he* and Jewel had never been anything other than friends. *Nor* had it ever crossed his mind that they could be. He'd been in a steady relationship for years. At least, up until a month ago. And even during the many times he and Bria had been "on a break" . . . Well, he couldn't say that Jewel had entered his mind during those times, either. She'd always just been Jewel.

Yet one look at Nick leaning into her, whispering something only she could hear, and white-hot spears of jealousy had shot through him.

What the heck?

He'd have to give that more thought later on. He was a man who often lived by intuition, and something shouted loud for him to pay attention to this one.

"So, what do you think?" Ashlee held two of his pieces up in front of her, elbows bent, leveling the carvings directly in front of her breasts. "Which one suits me the best? The deer" —she cocked her head to the right—"or the cute little sheep?"

Her lips pouted slightly as she waited for his answer, and he reminded himself that he wasn't looking to hook up with Ashlee, good-looking as she might be. He wasn't looking to hook up with *anyone*. He'd be home for five weeks, then he'd head back to school. *That* was what he had to focus on. His future.

"Is that sheep wearing wolf's clothing?" The question came from her left, and Bobby couldn't help the quick chuckle that slipped out as Jewel sidled up beside Ashlee. She offered an innocent grin to both of them. "Hi, Bobby. Ashlee."

Ashlee mumbled something that might have been a hello but sounded more like a less-polite greeting. A perturbed look settled onto her face.

"Hey, Jewel." Bobby's gaze soaked her in. Brunette hair was pulled to the back of her head. Gray-brown eyes that were trimmed in green twinkled out from a halo of long thick lashes. And there wasn't a speck of makeup anywhere to be found. She was refreshing and real.

She was the complete opposite of Bria.

"I think I'll take them both," Ashlee announced, speaking loud enough to capture the attention of customers from the next booth over. She clearly didn't like the focus not being on her, so she'd taken it back. She handed the carvings and a debit card over with a beaming smile before turning to Jewel and crossing her arms under her breasts. The move lifted her assets, causing her shirt to gape even more, while her eyes narrowed the tiniest amount. The smile remained on her face. "How's the *bull* business, *Jewel?*"

Bobby's brows hiked as he rang up the purchases, but he didn't say anything. Derision rang from Ashlee's tone. Either she was unimpressed with Jewel's career choice or she didn't care for bulls. Or both. Or maybe she simply disliked Jewel that much.

Didn't matter. None of those options would earn another glance from him, even if he'd wanted to give her one.

"The bull business is terrific," Jewel replied. "So far, we're on track to have the greatest season the Double B has seen in years, and I can only see that continuing. How's Mateo?"

The abrupt question had Ashlee taking a half step back and her smile—and arms—dropping. A pink flush crept across her cheeks, and she glanced at Bobby before answering. "Mateo is *fine.*" The last word pushed out from between gritted teeth.

"You two are still dating, aren't you?" Jewel didn't so much as blink as she volleyed the next question. She then looked around as if to seek out the other man. "I haven't seen him today. Did he not come with you?"

"Mateo had to work today," Ashlee returned.

"Ah."

Bobby held in his smile as the two women fell silent, but his mind worked overtime. Had Jewel come over simply to run Ashlee off? Because it certainly seemed like it. And if she had . . . what did that mean? Or did it mean anything?

Did he *want* it to mean something?

The questions ran rampant, and he tucked them away for later consideration, same as he had the jealousy issue. This was a whole new thing for him, and he didn't yet know what to make of it. Jewel?

He tossed another glance her way. He could certainly do worse.

Not that he was looking to *do* anything, he reminded himself.

These five weeks were a time for reflection and preparation for his future. Nothing more. He likely wouldn't even work in the studio his mom had let him set up back in high school. He would hang out with his mother when she wasn't busy at the hospital—she was an anesthesiologist, so she stayed busy far more often than not. He would spend time catching up with old friends. And he'd help at the Double B. That's all. And in five weeks, he'd start the next chapter in his life.

Bobby finished wrapping Ashlee's purchases and tucked them into a bag, and as she took the offering, she tossed out one last smile. It didn't make it to her eyes, however. Her irritation was clear. She'd been caught and called out, and she didn't appreciate it at all.

"Have a good day, Bobby."

He nodded. "You, too."

She left without another word, or so much as a glance in Jewel's direction, and he and Jewel both watched until she'd disappeared into the gathering throng of people. The cherry spitting contest would be starting in ten minutes, and a large number of festival goers were now making their way to the spitting "arena."

Once Ashlee could no longer be seen, Bobby turned back to Jewel and waited for her to look his way. And when she did . . . he totally let his grin stretch wide.

"What?" she demanded.

He couldn't take his eyes off her. "I can't believe you just did that."

"Did what?" She lowered her gaze to fidget with some invisible irritant that suddenly seemed to be bothering her palm.

"*Uhhh*," he drew the word out, hoping she would look back up, but she only continued to scratch at her hand. So, he dipped his head to hers. "Jewel Jackson, you totally just cock-blocked me with Ashlee."

Her gaze shot up. "What? No I did not."

With a knowing look, he merely stared back, and danged if her own cheeks didn't take on an adorable shade of pink.

"Stop it." She shoved at his shoulder. "I didn't 'cockblock' you. I was just . . ." Her words trailed off when he simply kept looking at her. And smiling. And as they stood there staring at each other, he decided that he liked both her boldness and her embarrassment. He'd always appreciated her boldness. That was one of the reasons his dad had hired her full time right after graduation.

Even as a teen, she would set her mind to something and wouldn't back down. And most times, those decisions paid off. It was one of the reasons they currently had a bull in their stock who would likely win them big money before this season was over. Jewel had sought out the right genetics to breed Rolls Royce, and she'd badgered his father until the man had agreed to it.

But the embarrassment was new. He wasn't sure he'd ever witnessed that before.

"You just, what?" he whispered.

The blush disappeared as quickly as it had come, and she pulled her shoulders back. She shot him a look of disgust. "Quit teasing me, Bobby Brandon. I was doing *you* a favor. You should thank me."

"Oh, really?"

"Yes, really. You haven't been around a lot over the last few years, so you may not be up to speed, but Ashlee Anderson has men for dinner these days and spits out nothing but bone when she's finished. Plus"—she jutted her chin out—"she's currently dating someone."

"Yeah." He nodded. Had she always been this adorable? "I picked up on that. Mateo. And *thank you*," he added, stressing the words she'd claimed he owed her. "I'd not only hate to get on this Mateo's bad side by simply talking to his girlfriend, but I'd be equally disgruntled to wake up tomorrow as nothing but bones."

She smirked. "You think you're cute, don't you?"

He stroked his hand over his recently grown beard. "Ashlee sure thought I was."

"Oh, for crying out loud."

He burst into laughter at both her words and the exaggerated eye roll, and if they weren't separated by the counter, he'd have wrapped her in a huge hug. "God, Jewel." He leaned on the counter, narrowing the gap between them. "I've missed you. You've always been such a bright light in my life."

14

The words sent her annoyance packing, and he once again found himself smiling at her. And this time, she smiled back. The festival noises surrounding them faded as he again asked himself why he'd been so jealous at seeing her talking to Nick. And why he wanted to believe she'd come over just now as much for herself as to "save" him.

"I do appreciate the rescue," he told her. She hadn't looked away. "Not that I really needed it, though. I had no intention of doing anything with Ashlee."

"No?"

"No."

They both fell silent, and he had the thought that if anyone happened to look their way, they might think the two of them were about to kiss. But he didn't care. Because he *wanted* to kiss Jewel. And he didn't want to second-guess it.

"I suppose you weren't going to do anything with Ashlee because of Bria, right?"

Damn. That brought the moment to a halt. But not because hearing his ex's name bothered him. Which was excellent.

He pulled back, putting space between them, then he picked up one of his favorite carvings. A bull. Every bull he made always had him thinking of Jewel.

"*Not* because of Bria." He didn't do anything with the miniature animal. He just held on to it.

"Why not?"

"Because we're done."

"Right."

"Yes. *Right.*" He nodded as if to prove himself. "For good this time."

Jewel studied him a moment longer, likely thinking "I've heard that before," then her brows hitched up. But Bobby didn't back down. He and Bria *were* finished. When he'd ended things, after she'd once again suggested they take yet another break, he'd worried he might come to regret that decision. That their breakup would hurt for more than the somewhat few days it had. After all, the two of them had dated on and off for almost nine years. He'd once thought her his soulmate.

But something had changed in the last year. Specifically, after his dad died. When he'd needed to be with his family, to help at the Double B instead of immediately jumping back into school. When Bria could barely hang around for two days after they'd put his father into the ground. Things had been different since then.

And when he'd corrected Bria in that moment a little over a month ago, stating that no, in fact, they weren't going to take another break. That they were *finished* instead. The biggest weight had lifted from his chest.

Jewel studied him for another moment, thinking whatever it was she might be thinking, then she gave a single nod. "I'm sorry," she said. "That must have been hard."

Relief washed through him. She believed him—or, at least, she wanted to. And that mattered for some reason.

He set down the bull he suddenly found himself gripping. "Not as hard as you might think."

CHAPTER THREE

Not as hard as she might think?

Jewel continued to let Bobby's words run on repeat the following Monday as she watched her two employees round up the younger bulls. Angi and Daniel were both high school aged, and both had been bumped to full-time hours while Leon was out on leave. Leon, hired from a nearby ranch last fall, was worth every dime he earned. And then some. But she, Angi, and Daniel could manage for the next few weeks. With Bobby's help over the weekends, of course.

And since she was now thinking of Bobby again, she couldn't help but hear his words one more time. And she still didn't understand. Why would breaking up with someone he'd been with his entire dating life not be "as hard as she might think?"

She knew he'd loved Bria. Everyone knew that.

He'd loved her since he'd first laid eyes on her in the sixth grade. Everyone knew *that*, as well. That love had been proclaimed throughout junior high, and once they'd finally gotten together—at the basketball homecoming dance their freshman year—Bobby's love at first sight story had become a part of *their* story.

But suddenly, he could simply walk away and it was no big deal?

She doubted it.

As she'd told Nick on Saturday, she would believe it when she saw it. Chances were Bobby would be back with Bria before summer's end, and she'd do good to keep that thought forefront in her mind. Otherwise, she might start having *other* thoughts. Like about the way Bobby had been staring at her at the festival after announcing his breakup.

How it had seemed he'd wanted to kiss her.

Because it had, right?

She was almost certain.

And if he *had* leaned in . . .

She shook her head, realizing just where her mind had gone yet again. She could *not* be having such thoughts. She couldn't harbor delusions where Bobby Brandon was concerned because he would never be hers.

"Eight o'clock sharp, boss." Bobby's voice came from behind her, causing her to spin in his direction. "Reporting for duty." He shot her a salute and a smile . . . and she gawked.

That beard . . .

That hair . . .

The cowboy hat held in his hands just waiting to go atop all of it.

She gulped. She wanted to curl her fingers into his mess of hair, pull him in close, and press her entire body up next to his. She wanted to—

Grrr. Stop!

Dang it, what was wrong with her? Just because Bobby was

the fantasy come to life that she hadn't known existed didn't mean she had to act on it—or even think about it. She was the manager of the Double B for heaven's sake. The head woman in charge of a stock contracting company that all Montana rodeos currently had their eyes on. The Double B had some impressive pedigree on their ranch at the moment. The best in a decade.

What she *wasn't* was a simpering female sitting around waiting for a sexy man to show up and sweep her into his arms. One to smile down at her and to—

She clamped down her thoughts yet again. This was stupid.

"Reporting for duty?" she asked, forcing her mind to the moment at hand, and proud of the calm that shone through in her voice. What was Bobby doing down at the barn, anyway? She hadn't expected to see him again until Friday.

"Leon is out," he explained. "So, I'm in."

She blinked. When his dad had fallen from the ladder the summer before, in a simple task gone bad, Bobby had stepped in until they'd recruited Leon. But he'd helped out *only* on weekends. During the rodeos.

He'd occasionally wandered the property throughout that time, occasionally making it down to the barn or one of the pens—when he hadn't been burrowed away in the apartment over the garage. But in all that time, the shadows filling his eyes never so much as hinted "put me to work." So instead, she'd taken the time to chat with him. She'd taken walks with him.

Through laughter and smiles, often by sharing stories about his dad, she'd done her best to help him step outside of his sorrow, even if only for a few seconds. And in doing so, those conversations had helped her to work through her own grief, as well. Because Blake Brandon had been more than a boss to her. He'd been her mentor. He'd been her friend.

Bobby, his entire family, and *she*, may have been reeling the year before. But if he *wanted* to work this time around?

Done.

She looked at her watch and held back a teasing grin. "Then you're late. Leon gets to work at six a.m." She looked him up and down. "You forget how early life starts on a ranch, city boy?"

One side of his mouth crooked up. "I didn't forget." He pushed the hair back off his forehead, and Jewel's toes curled inside her boots. "I had breakfast with Mom first."

The words landed an immediate hit to her heart.

"She didn't have an early surgery today," he went on. "And she still misses breakfasts with Dad. So . . ." He shrugged, and Jewel lost all attempt at sternness. She wanted to reach out and touch him instead. But not in a sexual way this time.

"You're still a momma's boy, aren't you, Bobby?"

There were three Brandon children, but Bobby was the baby. And honestly, given the age gap between him and his two siblings, he'd been as much a daddy's boy as he was his momma's. Both parents had doted on him.

"I prefer to think of it as me being the favorite," he corrected.

"Nope." She shook her head, and her tone went melancholy. "Just a sweetheart who would do anything for those he loves."

∾

BOBBY EYED JEWEL, but he didn't voice his words. She got him. And that astounded him. Simply put, she understood who he was and what he was about. Without her, he'd still be drowning in grief. What he didn't know, however, was why he hadn't seen that before. Jewel had been his savior the year before. He'd come home, ready to be here for his mother, to help out in place of his dad. And he'd almost sank to the bottom of the ocean with his own hurt.

He hadn't returned to Missoula until after the first of the year, staying the extra time for his mom, who'd shared a special kind of love with his dad. Or heck, maybe the extra time had all been for him. After revamping the studio over the garage to include a small living space, as well, he'd holed himself up for months. He'd needed the outlet to create. To be himself. He'd needed a respite before going back to reality. And he'd needed Jewel. Only, he hadn't known it.

She'd pulled him through the worst days of his life, made him feel good in the middle of often crushing pain. And he didn't know if he'd even thanked her for it.

Plopping his hat on his head now, he looked away from what suddenly seemed like all-knowing eyes. "I'll be sure to show up on time tomorrow, boss. What's on the agenda for today?"

"Keep calling me boss, for one," she mumbled under her breath, and the subtle undertones in her voice had him quickly glancing her way again. But she'd shifted her gaze.

She slipped on a pair of reflecting sunglasses, the wrap-around Oakleys making him think far more thoughts than merely being jealous of her talking to another man, and she nodded toward the now-full pen of bulls. "Today we practice. You can be the gateman."

A baseball cap appeared on her head in the next second, and like a well-oiled team, she and her staff got to work.

A couple of hours later, Bobby was exhausted but exhilarated. He'd pulled the gate open for each bull after Jewel had strapped them with a mechanical dummy and a flank strap, and he was impressed with the quality of those coming up through the ranks. The animals they were working with today were in training. Bulls were either born with a bucking instinct or not, and the majority of these seemed to have what it took. Some had higher intensity than others, their kicks and spins better. Yet, the most impressive sight of the morning had been Jewel.

The woman was in her element, and she knew it. Each move was made with confidence. Each decision based a little on intuition and a lot on knowledge of these four-legged athletes. And Bobby couldn't get over the way she seemed to "speak" with each bull as they waited their turn.

The last one got loaded in, and due to earlier comments, he knew this was the bull she'd been waiting for.

"Death Comes to Your Door," Jewel said, though she spoke to no one.

She didn't immediately strap the fifteen-pound dummy on the bull nor loop the flank strap around the back side of him. Instead, she quietly eyed him through the rungs of the chute. The bull stared back. Then she reached a hand through and put her fingers to his nose. A light smile touched her lips.

"You're going to be the best someday," she said, this time clearly speaking to the bull. "You're my favorite, aren't you, Death?"

The bull peered back, quiet in the small confines, as if he knew this were a moment not to be interrupted.

"You're going to make the Double B a lot of money. You're going to announce loud and clear that *I* know what I'm doing." She caressed her hand along the line of his nose. "And you're going to make me fall in love with this sport all over again."

Bobby found himself as mesmerized as the bull seemed to be. They all stood silent a few seconds longer, and he had the thought that he wanted to create a sculpture of her exactly like that.

Then in the next moment, everything changed. Determination filled Jewel's hazel eyes as she stepped up onto the second rung of the chute, and with easy movements, she slid the flank strap over Death. Hooking the rope from beneath, she pulled it up but didn't tighten it yet. It lay looped and just loose enough that it wouldn't fall back to the ground. Death bucked. He was primed and already ready to go. Then Jewel repeated similar movements with the mechanical dummy.

The box was made to simulate a rider, and once strapped on would have a pin that attached to the flank strap. When the gate was opened, Death would buck, trying to rid himself of his "rider," until Jewel used the remote to simultaneously release both dummy and strap, thus rewarding Death with a "win."

Bobby had seen this very action throughout his life. His dad, a retired bull rider, had started the Double B before he'd been born, and like his two older siblings, Bobby had grown up immersed in the business. Also, like his siblings, Bobby had never had any real desire to go into the business.

But watching Jewel now . . . seeing her love for the very animals that his dad had always been so passionate about . . . He found himself second-guessing why he'd followed his mother and siblings into the medical field.

The sport was intense, and the money potential excellent. However, the money *wasn't* a given.

His mother was an anesthesiologist, his brother a general surgeon, and his sister had specialized in otolaryngology. All big moneymakers.

He?

Well, he hadn't wanted to be in surgeries nor to see patients day in and day out. At least, not in the traditional sense. So, he'd chosen pharmacy. He liked the science of medications, and the job would provide a nice income, as well. What he didn't like, however, was the hours he'd likely work upon graduation.

Most pharmacy careers were in retail, and those could bring some long weeks. He and Bria had always determined it would be worth it, though, as it would provide the kind of life-style they'd once imagined.

But now, as he couldn't pull his eyes from Jewel, he found himself wanting to be more a part of *this* world.

She nodded, and he yanked open the gate, and Death was off.

His kicks were high, the extension of his back legs good. His spins were exactly what a judge—and a bull rider—would want to see. And Bobby knew that Jewel was right. Death would not only make the Double B good money, but he would also give Jewel credibility—not that she didn't already have it. The riders, some of whom occasionally trained here at the ranch, studied the Double B's animals well before meeting up with them. And like Jewel, they had their eyes on those coming up in a few years, as well. He'd seen all of that last summer, and he had no doubt it was still true. Especially given the stock competing for the Double B that season.

The dummy and strap dropped from around Death, and the bull did as he was supposed to and headed for the exit. Angi and Daniel immediately went into action, readying to return Death and the rest of the yearlings to their pasture, and leaving Bobby and Jewel alone in the now-empty practice pen.

Bobby turned back to Jewel to find her standing inside the chute, and a jolt of awareness shot through him. Fierceness glowed from her eyes. It was pride. And he understood.

Death was another bull bred, thanks solely to her. After Rolls Royce, Bobby knew his dad hadn't asked questions when she'd come to him with an idea. Jewel was some sort of bull whisperer in the stock contractor world, and they were lucky to have her.

And he found himself now *wanting* her.

"Death is spectacular," he said. He draped his arms over the gate as he pushed it closed with an audible *click*. They stood face-to-face. "Fierce and fiery. And freaking amazing."

Her gaze flicked over his.

"Kind of like his creator," he whispered.

He caught a tiny telltale sign of attraction. Her pupils dilated. And though he didn't know what might be about to happen, he was down for whatever.

She didn't back away. She didn't step out of the chute.

Instead, her chin inched up. "Are you flirting with me, Bobby Brandon?"

He smiled. He did love her boldness. "I would certainly *like* to flirt with you, Jewel Jackson."

Her eyes went even darker, and as she had a moment before, she studied him. She didn't respond immediately, and he could see her thoughts working. He wanted to lean the additional few inches and put his mouth to hers, but he wouldn't do it. Not without an invitation. But he might eventually beg for an invite.

Finally, she spoke. And she shook her head. "Don't do that to me. You'll be back with Bria soon, and I don't want to get in the middle of that."

He didn't point out that during the many times he and Bria had taken a break, they'd always had an understanding. They'd been free to date other people. Not that he'd taken that opportunity very often. None of that mattered now, because he *wasn't* getting back with Bria.

He didn't break eye contact. "I told you. She and I are finished."

"And I told you, I don't believe you."

She pulled away then, climbing up the back railing and slinging both legs over, but she looked back at him instead of hopping to the ground. The space between them now was the width of a bull.

"And anyway," she continued, her tone lighter, "if you two really were finished, the last thing I'd want is to be your rebound girl."

He sensed that she wanted him to smile. To laugh. She was attempting to turn the moment humorous to relieve the tension. But he didn't want to let it go.

"You'd never be a rebound girl for me, Jewel."

Her chin inched up. "Yeah?"

"Yeah."

"Why?"

He opened his mouth to answer, sensing that she truly wanted to hear what he had to say. But he wasn't quite certain *what* to say. Because he just *knew*? Because she was *her*?

Nothing sounded like more than any trite line any man might feed any woman.

She stood her ground. "What would make you want to flirt with me now anyway?" All teasing dropped from her words. "After all this time? Even if you have broken up with Bria for good. You've known me since we were kids. Why the sudden interest?"

That he could answer. "Because you were there for me last year."

She waited, clearly needing more.

"You were there for me from day one," he continued. "There for my family. For my mom. You were the friend I needed when I was stumbling around trying to find myself. You never backed away."

Hell, she'd *come* for him.

She would see him watching her working with the bulls. He'd be standing several hundred feet away, simply watching, trying to figure out if he should go down to help, go back "home" to Missoula, or if he should head to the cemetery where they'd buried his father and beg forgiveness for not being around much over the last few years.

It hadn't just been the loss of his father that had broken him, but the loss of the love his parents had shared. He'd always cherished that love. They had so much pride in each other, such respect and admiration. He wanted that same thing for himself. Yet, in the blink of an eye, because of one misstep, his father had been gone and his mother was left alone. Life could be so unfair.

And though he'd known Jewel had been busy each of those times she'd caught him watching her—she'd been working with one man down, after all—she'd still come to his side. Every time. Kind of like he could see her doing now.

With her legs slung back over the railing, she returned, not stopping until she and he once again stood face-to-face. And then her eyes took on a soft haze. "Of course I was there for you, Bobby," she whispered. "You were hurting. You needed someone."

He nodded. "And that's why, Jewel. That's why I suddenly see you differently. I never thought about it before, but I have recently."

He'd thought about it all weekend, in fact. Ever since he'd wanted to ram a fist into Nick Wilde's face. She'd been the girlfriend his own girlfriend hadn't been for him. She'd allowed him to get through that time and come out somewhat whole on the opposite side.

"So, yes." He lifted a hand and cupped her cheek before lightly dragging a finger down to her bottom lip. "I do want to flirt with you, Jewel. I want to do more than that."

CHAPTER FOUR

I do want to flirt with you, Jewel. I want to do more than that.

Once again, Jewel found Bobby's words running on repeat. He'd uttered those sentences four days ago, and fear had lodged in her chest. She'd wanted him to flirt with her, too. She wanted more than that, *too*.

But at what cost?

Or maybe there wouldn't be a cost? Couldn't they simply have a summer fling before he went back to Bria? She'd certainly crushed on him for long enough. Most girls would jump at the opportunity.

But she'd told him she needed to think about it.

She needed time to make sure she could handle it if it turned into more.

The last thing she wanted was to be hurt come the end of summer, and if any man was capable of hurting her, Bobby would be that person.

She'd given him her thoughts, then she'd suggested he find something else to do for the remainder of the day. He'd taken her suggestion, but at exactly six o'clock the following morning—and each subsequent morning thereafter—he'd reported in for "work." And he'd also flirted each day. Not a lot, but enough to have her looking forward to whatever he might say next. Enough to have her tossing the occasional flirt back.

It had been a good week. A fun week. At least until today.

Bobby had been different today. They'd driven five hours in the truck together, not to mention loading and unloading the bulls, and there had been no easy banter. No teasing. In fact, he'd almost seemed aloof.

Had he changed his mind? Had Bria already gotten back under his skin?

Stepping from the building that housed the public showers, she pushed her wet hair back from her face and headed toward the camping area to find out. During rodeo season, the entire group who made up the sport became more family than individual. Stock contractors, bull riders, bull fighters, as well as spouses and kids often hung out together in the evenings, and usually even camped together. She and Bobby had only three bulls with them that weekend, so they'd brought the trailer that had a separate living space. It contained two beds, each in its own room, and she had absolutely no idea how the night might go.

"Rolls Royce," one of the riders called out as she returned to camp. Several others sent up a cheer.

She grinned. "You got that right." Rolls was unridden this season, and every rider there both wanted to draw his name, for a potential higher score, and dreaded having to ride him.

She lowered to the tree stump next to Bobby, the soft cotton of the leggings she'd changed into rubbing against his rougher jeans as she settled into place, and without a word, he handed over a block of wood and a knife.

Comfort eased through her. This was how they'd spent evenings the summer before. Bobby had taught her how to hand carve several animals throughout those weeks, and while the group chatted and wound down from the days, she and Bobby whittled.

"I'd forgotten about this." She spoke softly, for his ears only. "Thank you."

"My pleasure."

The simple words, spoken in his low, slightly gruff voice, sent goosebumps skittering over her body. "Did I miss anything while I was gone?"

Bobby nodded toward Nick and the woman now curled up at his side. "Betsy showed up."

Betsy was a buckle bunny well known in the Montana rodeo world.

"Good for him." As she said the words, she glanced back over at Bobby, and it was as if that moment at the cherry festival was happening all over again. The moment when she'd first thought he wanted to kiss her. He didn't look away; she held her breath. She *wanted* this man to kiss her. She *wanted* to do more.

But then he blinked, and the moment was gone.

"I've got to tell you something." His tone sounded shameful, and his eyes went blank, and she immediately nodded.

Here it comes, she thought. He's back with Bria.

Girding her emotions, and angry with herself for even thinking about sleeping with the man, she forced out her next words. "Tell me." She'd known this would happen. Anger sliced through her.

31

But instead of replying, Bobby's still-vacant gaze slipped past hers, and when it landed on something behind her and then locked on tight, the back of her neck began to itch. What was she missing?

Turning, she scanned the area. "What is it?"

"Easup," he muttered beside her. "He's a fucking asshole."

Jewel's eyes popped. Bobby rarely cursed.

After firing a glance back at Bobby, she studied Easup. One of the other stock contractors, Adrien Easup, stood on the opposite side of the campfire, a beer in one hand and a self-sure grin on his mouth. He spoke with one of the older riders, wearing the air of confidence she often associated with him. And he had reason to be confident. He'd had the best bulls in the business for the last several years. That was due only to the rough patch the Double B had gone through, of course. Before that, Bobby's dad had always run neck and neck with Easup, sometimes easing ahead of the other man, other times falling behind. It had been years of healthy competition, but if ever there were a nemesis to the Double B, Adrien Easup was it.

She turned back to Bobby.

"Let's walk." He rose, holding a hand down for her, and she took it without question.

"What's going on?" she asked the minute she was on her feet.

Bobby didn't reply. He simply led them away. Once they'd put a hundred feet between them and the rest of the group, he finally released her. But he didn't look her way.

"Bobby?" Worry settled inside her. "What is it? What happened?"

He pulled off the hat he'd worn all week and ran a hand through his hair. And as he did, he stared over her shoulder as if once again seeking out the man in question. She peeked back at Easup, as well.

"What did he do?" she demanded, and when she turned back, cold eyes finally latched on to hers. She'd never seen Bobby so angry.

"He made an offer to buy the Double B."

CHAPTER FIVE

B obby peered through the magnifier and focused on the intricacy of the project in front of him. It would be a character from a Japanese manga series when finished, and it was about three-fourths complete. He'd started it when he'd been home the year before, wanting to try something new that he couldn't do in his smaller workspace in Missoula. So, he'd looked up a popular series, made a few sketches, and off he'd gone.

As he worked now, he tried yet again to put the last couple of days behind him. Or, at least, to shed the bad parts of the weekend. Rolls Royce had remained unridden, so that had been good. At least, it should have been a positive. But as it was, Rolls going unridden would only encourage Easup to up his offer. Which, in turn, would leave his mother more inclined to sell.

He gritted his teeth and reminded himself to focus on the good stuff. The positives. Such as *Jewel*.

Jewel, he was finding out, was always a positive. She calmed him. She made him smile.

She got him.

Even when he was so damned furious he saw nothing but red, Jewel had a way of soothing him.

Unfortunately, being that angry—and then sharing the news with her—had *not* led their weekend down the path he'd originally hoped. In a strange way, however, it *had* made them closer. Which was nice. They'd seethed together over the injustice of losing a part of their lives that meant so much, and without even being able to fight for it.

And losing it to Easup.

Her jaw had gone slack the instant he'd shared the news.

"I had no idea your mom wanted to sell. When did that happen?"

"She wasn't looking to. At least, according to her. But he approached her with an offer, and she wants us to consider it."

Tears had sprung to her eyes.

"But it's your dad's business. His passion."

And yeah, he knew that. *And* he knew that his mother had always been so proud of all her husband's accomplishments. They'd both been supportive of each other. Always had the other's backs. Yet one crap offer by the one man his dad would never have wanted to sell to, and that was all it took?

He ground his teeth and refocused on his work.

He did *not* want to sell.

"Is it a done deal?" Jewel asked. "A good offer?"

"No, and no."

They hadn't even gotten into the fact that it would leave *her* unemployed. Not that she couldn't find another job. Anyone in the business would jump at the chance to hire her. But these were her bulls as much as they'd been his dad's, and it had made him sick to give her the news.

"Mom wants us all to agree," he told her. "Yes or no. After Dad

died, the business was split between the four of us. But Brady and Brooklyn won't ever be a part of it. They're solid in their careers, and both live a couple hours away. Selling won't matter to them. Mom is always busy." He shrugged. "And now I'm . . ."

"About to start a whole new life for yourself, as well."

"Yeah." Which, some days, royally sucked.

"But"—her eyes implored his—"does it have *to be Easup?"*

That had been the million-dollar question. Did it have to be fucking Easup? He hadn't asked that of his mom. He'd been too shocked and pissed right out of the gate. And he hadn't talked to her since. He and Jewel had done their jobs at the rodeo, then they'd returned without talking about it again. The drive home had been ridiculously silent, neither of them being up to conversation. He'd left her at the barn several hours ago, and he'd been snarling at his manga project ever since.

A knock sounded at his door, and he scowled instead of getting up. He still didn't want to talk to his mother. He didn't want to say the things to her that were on his mind.

Did she not love Dad anymore?

How could she possibly move on so soon?

How could she simply toss his dad's legacy aside?

When the knock sounded again, he growled and set his tools down. Turning off the light on the magnifier, he slipped a cloth over the sculpture and rose. His mom knew that he did more than the simple carvings he sold at the festival and in the shop downtown. He'd given her a figurine of a man and a woman a couple of years ago. The woman was in scrubs and the man in a cowboy hat. But even she didn't know how much *more* he did. No one did. And he wasn't about to share that information now, either.

Stomping across the room, he wrenched open the door, deciding to let it out. Blast his mother with all his thoughts. Only, it wasn't his mom standing at the top of his stairs. It was Jewel. And she still looked as furious as him.

"HOW BAD WAS THE OFFER?" Jewel demanded without waiting for him to speak.

"What?"

She pushed her way into the small living space. "I asked the other night if it was a good offer, and you said no. So, how bad was it?" She braced her hands on her hips. "Did he offer what Rolls is worth?"

"No."

"So then, not what Death is going to be worth, either?"

"Correct."

"Then I don't get it, Bobby." She paced across the floor before turning back. "Why would your mom even consider it? Am I not doing a good enough job running things?"

Was that what she thought?

"Jewel." He reached for her, but she ignored him and kept pacing. "*No*," he insisted. "You're doing an amazing job, and Mom knows it. We all know it. The Double B wouldn't be the same without you."

"Then why sell?" She stopped moving and glared at him. "Why get rid of everything that your dad—" Her voice cracked, and danged if tears didn't appear in her eyes again.

Pain filled Bobby, finally making him see something other than anger. He hurt for her. He hurt for *himself*. And he hurt for his mother, who even though she claimed she was fine with selling, he worried she might come to regret it.

He forced himself to admit the truth. "She's selling because of me."

And that was his biggest issue. His mother was willing to sell what had meant the most to his dad—*to her husband*—because of him.

Anger eased from Jewel's face, replaced by confusion. "Because of you?"

He sighed. Then he hid all other emotions. "She thinks that by keeping the Double B, by keeping *Dad's* dream, it'll interfere with *mine*."

"How?"

He stared at her. He didn't want to answer. Because when he did, he knew she'd take that burden on herself.

"Bobby." She moved to him. "I'm running the business. You're about to go back to school. How would selling it help *you*?"

"Because I didn't go to school *last* year."

It took a moment, but reality hit. He saw it with her involuntary step back. Then he watched as the color drained from her face. "And then Leon needed off this summer . . . and you had to come home again."

"Right."

"But you'll be done in time to start school this time. Leon will be back on the job."

He didn't say anything else. He waited for her to figure it out. It didn't take long.

"But what if it happens again?" she said, her voice growing softer. "What if you're needed *again*?"

He swallowed. "Right. That's Mom's argument. It's not always easy to find last-minute help."

"Then I coerce one of my sisters into helping." Fierceness filled her. "Or maybe all three of them. They could rotate. That's what family is for, after all. Heck, that's what I should have insisted on doing this time."

He let out a sad laugh. And while he appreciated her energy, her willingness to twist her sisters' arms, he knew it wouldn't change his mother's mind. She'd stated as much when he'd offered the same suggestion. She'd refused to hear him when he'd said that it had been *his* choice to stay home the year before. His choice to delay school.

"She's made her mind up," he told her, letting her see his acceptance of the situation. "We all have to agree, but none of us will go against her wishes. If she decides to sell, we'll sell."

"But for less than it's worth?"

He shook his head at that. "No. That we *won't* agree on, and neither will she. She told Easup she'd take another offer Labor Day weekend. At the end of the summer's competitions. That'll give both sides time to truly evaluate what Rolls is worth. What Death will be worth. Not to mention, the rest of the bulls, the equipment, the *name*."

Horror suddenly shown on her face. "The land?"

"Not the land," he confirmed. "Not the house. She won't do that. She might lease out the land at some point, though."

"Good."

"But she is going to ask your opinion on our stock"—he shot her a raised brow and a teasing grin—"and I'm hoping you won't unfairly inflate the numbers?"

Annoyance filled her eyes. "Of course I won't unfairly inflate the numbers."

"Not even because it's Easup?"

That earned him a half smile and her signature eye roll.

"I may *want* to inflate the numbers," she clarified, "but no. If your mom really wants to sell, I'll do what I can to help. Plus, fucking Easup would know if I wasn't being legit anyway."

He chuckled. And then he grew silent. He took her hand. "And *you'll* be okay?"

Her gaze flickered to his.

"I know you could get another job," he continued, but he left unsaid that by doing so she'd be walking away from "her" bulls. From the business she'd put so much of her own self into.

She seemed to understand his question, but she didn't immediately answer. Instead, she once again began to pace. Only, she moved slower this time. She made it to the edge of the living room, took in his bed tucked into the nearest corner, the mini fridge and microwave crammed in beside a table barely large enough for one. Then as if in slow motion, her head turned, and she scanned the rest of the space.

The band saw, the chisels, the Dremel, the carving bits.

The shards of wood he hadn't cleaned up from the work he'd been doing today.

She also eyed the large locked cabinet sitting against the back wall and the piece, now covered, that he'd been working on before opening the door to her.

Taking another couple of steps forward, she peered around the edge of the workbench. He held his breath instead of stopping her. She'd not been in here before. No one had other than his mom. And even then, *she* had never seen half the pieces now on display. She didn't know all he was capable of.

"Bobby," Jewel whispered. He fingers went to her mouth. "I had no idea."

"No one does," he admitted. His heart hammered in his chest.

Bria knew he had more talent than the simple pieces he sold, but even she'd never understood how much. She also thought of this as his "little hobby."

"Welcome to my studio." The words were laced with the fear that she might not appreciate what she was looking at. What he was allowing her to see.

"All that time last year," she murmured.

She moved to the workbench and picked up the queen and king he'd made for a chess set. He had yet to paint them, but he soon would.

She held up the pieces. "*This* is what you were doing?"

He nodded. "It is."

"Then why in the world are you hiding it from everyone? Why isn't *this* your dream?"

The words, though something he'd asked himself before, felt like lead weights settling over him. "I can't make a living doing this."

"Are you sure?" She lifted the cloth from the manga piece and literally gaped as she pointed at it. "This is *insane*."

He smiled. He did appreciate her appreciation for his work.

"This is something to do in my spare time." He moved into the workshop area with her. "It's what I'll take up again after I retire."

The sharp look sent his way caught him off guard. "You're going to quit doing this now?" She sounded angry. "*Why?*"

"Because I won't have the time. Not once school starts.

And when I graduate"—he shrugged, not sure how to make her understand—"I'll likely end up working in retail. Pharmacist hours can be brutal."

"Then don't be a pharmacist," she muttered, and the way she said the words, the awe coloring her features, inflated his ego. It reminded him of how his parents used to look at each other.

She continued to seek out every nook and cranny, her eyes, as well as her fingers, taking everything in. "I don't know how you can*not* do it, Bobby. You clearly have a passion for this."

He'd wondered that same thing, as well. Especially after he'd worked so hard the year before to bring his skill to a new level. He wasn't sure he was ready to quit seeing where he could take things.

As she continued skimming her fingers over each piece, he decided to take one more risk. Why not fully go for it?

He reached for the key tucked behind the locked cabinet. "Do you want to see more?"

She spun in his direction. "You have more? *Yes.* Please!"

Without giving himself time to think about what he was doing, he slipped the key into the lock and pulled both doors open wide. Then he took a step back. These were the real pieces. The ones he'd envisioned seeing in art galleries. This was the type of artwork he wanted to spend his life improving upon.

The theme was the human body. Hands, faces, curves, shapes, nudes, partial nudes. He had women in yoga poses, women rising up out of water. Mother and child. Lovers standing back-to-back. He'd carved every pose that had ever spoken to him, every thought that made him *feel*. He'd smoothed and polished them until they were as close to perfection as he could get. And then he closed them up in a locked cabinet.

Jewel hadn't said anything yet. Nor had she made a sound.

And the eerie silence had Bobby's pulse racing.

Finally, he couldn't take it any longer. He slipped his hands into his jeans' pockets and rocked back onto his heels. "Say something."

She turned to him then, and the look on her face, the sheer understanding of what these pieces meant to him, had him falling a little bit in love with her. No one had ever looked at his work that way. No one had looked at *him* that way.

She didn't comment. Instead, with methodical movements, she slowly closed the doors, then pressing her back against the cool metal, she pulled a breath in through her nose. And finally, she spoke.

"Why did you break up with Bria?"

He jolted at the unexpected question, but once past the initial shock, found it interesting that's where she'd gone. It was as if she instinctively knew. "Because she didn't want me coming back here again. She was afraid I'd end up delaying school for another year."

She lifted her hand and touched one finger to the door behind her, right above her shoulder. "She was afraid you'd spend a few more weeks doing this?"

"She's never actually seen those. But yes. She's not a fan of my carvings."

She laughed. "Those are not *carvings*, Bobby. Those are *art*."

He wanted to hold this woman.

And he might never want to let go.

She looked around the room again, seeming to take in

everything around them, each ounce of his soul he'd put into the work, before finally bringing her gaze back to his. And when her gorgeous eyes once again zeroed in on him, the earth shifted beneath his feet.

"You made the right decision breaking up with her. Now, kiss me, will you? Before I go up in flames. Because for all those years that you saw only Bria, I saw only *you*. And I didn't even *know* about all of this."

Shock rooted him in place. She'd always liked him?

How had he not known that?

And his work made her like him even more? That was the sexiest thing she could have said.

He hesitated no longer and did exactly as she asked. And as his lips closed over hers, for the first time in his life, it felt as if he'd truly come home.

CHAPTER SIX

J ewel slid both arms around Bobby's neck and flattened her body to his, and she'd have scaled him like a tree if he hadn't lifted her up at the same time. Hands cupping her bottom, he pressed her to an impressively large erection. And with a grunt, he backed her into the cabinet.

Something fell over, but the sound slowed neither of them.

"Jewel." Bobby tugged at one of her knees, and she clamped both legs around him. He finished his thought with a groan.

"Bed," she uttered. It might be fun to be taken against a wall—or a cabinet—but she didn't want to risk breaking any of the pieces she'd just laid eyes on. "Hurry," she added, and he complied. And as she landed on the bed she'd eyed earlier, Bobby's shirt disappeared over his head.

She was about to have sex with Bobby Brandon, and oh, Lord, what was underneath his clothing seemed as if it was going to be just as delectable as what could be found on the outside.

"Come here." She held her arms out, wiggling her fingers in

desperation to touch him. For him to touch her. But he apparently had other ideas. Because instead of moving to her side, he suddenly slowed.

He unzipped his jeans. He kicked off his boots.

She panted in anticipation.

And then . . . he did nothing.

"What?" she begged. Her breathiness gave away her level of need, and she rose to her knees. Her chest heaved.

"You're still wearing all your clothes."

"Oh." She looked down, and a sly grin rose to her lips. The tip of her tongue touched her lip. "And you'd like me to take them off, I presume?"

She undid the top button of her shirt, her smile as naughty as his, but stopped when Bobby held up a hand. He shook his head. "I changed my mind."

Pure evil smiled out at her. A clump of hair had fallen forward, swooping down over one of Bobby's eyes, and he suddenly looked like a pirate, come to ravish her. A shiver racked over her body.

"Tell me what you want," she offered. She would do anything he asked.

"Over the couch." He didn't ask, he *told*. And her breath caught at the command. She could do over the couch. She could freaking *love* over the couch.

He nodded toward the only piece of furniture in the living room, his movements slow and his eyes never leaving hers, then he slipped one hand down the front of his jeans.

He stroked himself, and she went instantly wet.

She watched, frozen in place, as he gripped his length. He slowly stroked, his fist moving up and down, and she licked her lips. She nearly begged to put him in her mouth right then and there, but he seemed intent on other plans. And since she expected she'd get the opportunity to have *her* way with him later, she obeyed.

"The couch," she repeated and rose from the bed. Only, as she set one foot on the floor, she intentionally dragged her fingers over the seam of her jeans.

Bobby moaned.

"Clothes on or off?"

His eyes glittered. "Jeans undone. I'll take care of the rest."

She bit her lip. *Yes, sir!*

Her breathing didn't improve as she hurried to the couch, but as she moved, she also never took her eyes off him. He continued to stroke himself, and she could see that the tip of him now glistened.

"Bobby," she pleaded when she bent over the back of the furniture, pointed her tush in the air, and he didn't immediately follow.

"*Shhh*," he whispered. "Just stay right where you are. I'm enjoying the view."

She chuckled. But then she squirmed, wiggling her butt as she unbuckled and unzipped her jeans. She pushed them slightly down over the tops of her hips, and when she peeked back over her shoulder again, she could see that playtime for Bobby was nearing an end.

His eyes had darkened, and his chest now heaved, same as hers.

"Take me, Bobby," she begged. "I want you inside me. I've wanted you for years."

She didn't have to wait any longer. Bobby was behind her in an instant, his dick now out of his jeans and pressing between her still-clothed butt cheeks. His arms circled her, his fingers ripping at her shirt, until at least two of the buttons flew free. He was a wild man as he reached inside and palmed one breast. He dragged it from the lace of her bra and pinched her nipple hard.

Her knees went weak.

"*Shit*," she whispered. Her head dropped to his chest. "Hurry, Bobby. *Please*. Or I'm going to freaking come before you ever touch me."

He chuckled low and deep, the sound vibrating through her body. Then, with arms still surrounding her, he kept one hand at her breasts but slipped the other to the front of her jeans.

He slid inside her panties.

"Bobby!" she cried out at the first touch of his fingers. Her breasts ached. Her nipples hardened into painful peaks.

"I've got you, baby."

He continued to fondle her, his fingers aware of exactly where to touch and how long to linger, and she squirmed back against him. She needed this man inside of her.

"You're so fucking hot," he whispered as his other hand squeezed at her breasts.

His thumb flicked over a nipple, causing her to jerk, before he pinched down hard once again.

"*Fuck.*" She reared back, desperately wanting his mouth where his fingers were.

He nipped at the side of her neck and pinched the other nipple at the same time, and the most exquisite pleasure shot through her. Her knees weakened even more.

"I need to come, Bobby," she pleaded, the sound desperate and weak. She dropped her head to her chest and squeezed her eyes closed tight. "I need it so bad."

"Soon, baby." He kissed the back of her neck. "*Shhh*," he whispered. "Very soon."

His fingers slowed then, as if unwilling to give her the joy of an orgasm just yet. His touch transitioned into long, slow strokes, and she kept her eyes closed and rode high on the delicious moment. Her hips continued to move against him. Pushing back. Seeking more. And somehow, he even managed to slow *her* movements.

She seemed to float out of her body, and she wondered if she might pass out. But if so, would it be from pleasure or need?

And then Bobby changed things up yet again.

Suddenly, he removed his hands from her body and shoved her jeans and panties to the floor. He stood tall behind her and rolled a condom down over himself. As he did, she glanced back in anticipation, her breaths once again picking up, and she kicked one leg free of her clothes.

"Now?" she asked.

He nodded. His features were drawn tight. *"Now."*

Once protected, he bent her back over the couch, spread her legs with a knee, and then he was inside her.

They both gasped. Both arched.

"Oh, God." She shuddered.

He was big, and he filled her up. Her body stretched to accommodate him, and he began to move. But when she dropped her head to her chest again, focusing on her own movements as she met him thrust for thrust, he fisted a handful of her hair and tugged.

"Watch," he demanded.

She forced her eyes open as he pulled her head up, and what she hadn't noticed before now filled her vision. A television sat directly in front of them, no picture on the screen, and their image reflected back. Her breasts, spilling out the front of her shirt, and him like some freaking Viking warrior, pumping into her from behind, was the hottest thing she'd ever seen.

Her breasts jiggled every time he thrust, and she couldn't have looked away if she'd tried.

He slammed harder into her, and she whimpered with the beauty of it. With the pleasure of it. He kept his one hand on her hip, holding her where he wanted her and increased his speed. And as he pumped, as she ground back into him, their eyes met and held in their reflection.

"I like you like this," he told her. He leaned forward and nipped at her ear. "I fucking *love* you like this," he growled. Then he released her hair and slipped his fingers down the front of her body until they hovered over her center. "But before I let you come, you have to promise that we get to do this all over this damned apartment tonight."

She nodded, the movement jerky. That she could definitely promise.

"Say it," he grunted.

"I promise," she whimpered.

And then he sent her soaring.

CHAPTER SEVEN

H oly hell.

Jewel gulped as she kept her gaze on Bobby, who was currently making his way through the crowd on the opposite side of the arena, food and drinks held above his head. He smiled at whatever someone said as he passed them, and her heart thudded a little harder. The man remained as hot today as the night he'd first bent her over the couch. And she had as big a crush on him now as ever.

Four weeks.

It has been four sexy, hot, sleep-deprived blissful weeks.

They'd been together every night since that first one, and she still couldn't look at him without getting turned on. He was insane in bed.

No wonder Bria always came back. Hell, *she* probably would, too, if he'd let her.

She shook her head, knowing that wouldn't be the case. They'd agreed that this was a summer fling, and no more. Exclusivity while it lasted, but once his stint in Birch Bay was over, they would go their separate ways. He had his future to focus on, after all. And *she* would have a new job to find.

She sighed. At least, she assumed she'd have to find a job. Rolls Royce remained unridden and Easup still got the look of a man who'd grabbed hold of a brass ring any time he caught sight of one of her bulls.

However . . . She'd been having thoughts.

Nothing she'd talked to Bobby about yet because she wasn't sure she could pull it off, or if she wanted to. *Or* if he and his family would go for it if she did present her idea. But she'd definitely been having thoughts. And thoughts *other* than about what position they would try each night.

"Still ogling, I see."

She jerked at the sound of Nick's voice, then blushed bright as a tomato when she looked up at him.

"*Damn*," he murmured. "That good, huh?"

She elbowed him in the chest. "You startled me."

Nick knew that she and Bobby were together. Everyone knew it. They hadn't made it a secret. But she also hadn't talked about him with anyone. After all, they were just having a good time. She didn't want to start thinking it could be more.

"This is his last night?"

She nodded. Everyone also knew that Bobby would be staying in Missoula tonight. School would start back the following week. The rodeo this weekend was in his own town, so instead of camping out with the rest of the group, he'd driven down separately, and they planned to stay in his apartment tonight. Then tomorrow, she would go home alone.

Her throat grew tight at the thought. It hadn't just been

sex these last four weeks. She'd gotten to know him better, too. They'd talked, they'd laughed. They'd even gone on dates.

Once she'd seen the type of carvings he *really* did, she'd refused to let him work with her during the week, instead insisting he take whatever time he needed to focus on his art. And in return, he'd occasionally let her watch him in action. Which had then led to even more sex.

The man was hot when he was focused.

Hot, period.

And sweet and kind. And simply a good guy.

Her throat ached with the need to shed tears.

"You going to be okay?" Nick asked, and she realized she'd disappeared into her own thoughts.

"Of course." She forced a smile. "Why wouldn't I be?"

She was going to miss Bobby like crazy.

"Oh, I don't know. Because you're in love with the man?"

She didn't look at him. "Wrong. It's just lust."

"Uh-huh."

He quit talking as the next rider readied to climb into the nearest chute. Both of them watched. James Crawley had drawn one of Easup's bulls, and as he waited his turn, Jewel found herself seeking out Crawley's girlfriend. Bria's sister sat in the crowd, but thankfully Bria hadn't come with her. That had been a worry for Jewel, especially since Bria lived here. After all, it seemed about time the other woman would decide to reel Bobby back in.

"For the record," Nick whispered at her side, "I think he's got it bad for you, too."

She wiped an escaping tear away, but the lump in her throat remained.

"Are you really just going to let him go?"

"What choice do I have, Nick?" Her voice barely made it to her own ears, so she didn't know if Nick heard her or not. But when he slipped an arm around her, she leaned into him. Yep. Walking away from Bobby was going to hurt.

Crawley gave a nod once he'd settled onto the bull, and as the gate opened, Nick's arm fell away. They both leaned forward.

Eight seconds was all it took.

Eight seconds and eighteen-hundred pounds of muscle.

The numbers on the clock ticked off, and with just point three seconds to go, Crawley went down.

Nick blew out a shaky breath. "*Dang.* The man is too close for comfort."

She patted him on the arm. "You've got this. It's going to be your year."

"I sure hope so."

Circuit finals wouldn't be until January, when Montana's top riders would be crowned, but local competitions wrapped in two weeks. On Labor Day.

Which would be the same weekend she found out if she'd lost the Double B or not.

GRAY LIGHT OOZED around the edges of the blinds, letting Bobby know the forecast for the day had been correct. Cloudy and overcast. Just like his heart.

He glanced to the far side of the bed, careful not to disturb Jewel, to see that it was six fifteen. He would have to take her back to get the bulls soon. Only, he didn't know how he was going to let her go.

He'd just had the best four weeks of his life. Spent those weeks with the only woman he could imagine ever being with again.

Jewel was special. And he would be a shell of himself without her.

But he didn't know how to give them anything other than this last morning.

She stirred under the arm he'd slung over her, and he remained extra still. He was too raw for the day to begin. They hadn't gotten back to his place until after midnight, and though they'd come together as if they'd been doing it for years, their time together hadn't been enough.

Holding her now *wasn't* enough.

When her breathing changed from deep to shallow, he lifted his head and looked down. Solemn eyes stared back, making him wonder if she was having any of the same thoughts as he.

"Make love to me again?" he whispered. He refused to say "one last time." And when she nodded, he moved on top of her.

There were no sexual gymnastics this morning. No rush to reach orgasm.

They simply loved each other's bodies as if this would be the last time.

Cupping her face in his hands as he rocked in and out of her, he kissed her deep and long. As always, she was hot and wet, her insides clinging to him as if unwilling to let go. And she fit him perfectly. He wanted to keep this moment forever.

With no idea what else to do, he showed her without words what she meant to him, and he got the same in return. But all too soon, it was over. The sun rose. A sliver of brightness crept through the otherwise gloomy morning. And they were finished.

"I've got to shower." She spoke the words softly, rolling out of his arms at the same time.

Fifteen minutes later, she emerged from his bathroom, her hair wet and face impassive, and Bobby rose from the chair where he'd been waiting. He'd pulled his clothes from the night before back on, but hadn't bothered to comb his hair.

She held up her cell. "I called for a car. You don't have to take me."

His heart cracked. "Why?" He was supposed to have fifteen more minutes.

"There's no need to do this in front of other people, Bobby. We can say goodbye here."

She stood before him, her features stoic, and he had a moment of uncertainty. Was this as hard on her as it was him? Or had he only imagined it?

He honestly didn't know any longer.

Nodding, as if in agreement, and unsure what else to do, he took her bag and led her through the apartment. But when they made it the door, he didn't open it. He just stood there. They couldn't end like this. She was the only person who'd ever truly understood him. The one who saw that he wasn't fully alive unless he was working with wood.

She'd encouraged him to spend time in his studio these last four weeks, and that single act meant more than anything. He had to make sure she knew that.

Before he could find the words, she took her bag and reached for the door.

"Don't." He pushed his palm to the door, slamming it closed the instant it opened.

She looked up at him.

"Don't go, Jewel. Not like this. Let's keep dating."

"*Bobby.*" She didn't say anything more. And she didn't show any emotion.

His panic rose. "We're great together. You have to see that."

"I do see it. This has been a terrific few weeks. But this is what we agreed to."

"Fuck what we agreed to. We can change our minds."

She let out a short laugh. "And then what? We live over an hour from each other."

"It's *just* an hour." He didn't see what the big deal was. "We see each other on weekends. Whenever we can get away."

"That won't work."

He smacked the door with his palm again, and she jumped. "Why won't it work, Jewel? Was this honestly just sex for you?"

Her eyes took on an icy chill. "Don't you dare insult me by asking that question."

"You're insulting me by walking away." He pulled his hand down, telling himself to rein in his emotions. Anger wouldn't solve anything. But anger was about all he had left. "We *can* make this work. You know we can. We're only an hour apart."

She let her bag drop to the floor then, and she took his hands in hers. A hint of softness finally appeared in her eyes. "You'll be busy, Bobby. That's the issue. Too busy for me."

"I won't."

"You *will*. Wasn't it you who told me that the one thing you hold so dear, your woodworking, would have to be put to the side while you go to school? Possibly until you retire?" The softness was replaced by the original stoicism. "Where do I fit into that scenario? If you did find time to drive an hour each direction, I'd rather you spend it in your workshop than with me. I don't want you to lose that part of yourself."

Her words made sense, but at the same time . . . And then he had the solution.

"Move down here with me."

She looked stunned by his suggestion. "My job is—"

"Likely ending anyway."

Though she recoiled at his harsh words, he kept going.

"I'm just saying, if Mom *does* sell . . ." He gripped her hands tight. "Then move here with me. You can find a job here. Every stock contractor in the state knows you. Anyone would hire you. I'll go to school, you'll work, then once I've graduated—"

She stopped him with fingers to his mouth. Her eyes remained blank. "That isn't my dream, Bobby. It's yours." She pressed her lips together, her gaze dropping for a second and her fingers lowering. "It's yours and Bria's."

He shook his head. He didn't know what else to say.

"I'm not a replacement for the woman you've always wanted," she told him, picking her bag back up off the floor. "I'm not a stand-in, and I refuse to ever be one. Also, I have my own plans for my life."

"And what? Those plans can't include me?"

Fire flashed in her eyes. "What they *won't* include is me sitting around, waiting for you, only to see if you might someday still want *me*. Go back to Bria, Bobby. Live out the life you've always planned."

Fury grew inside him. "Don't do it, Jewel. Don't walk out that door."

"Or what?"

He shook his head. Too many years of letting Bria yank

him back and forth finally caught up with him. "I'm not going to have another relationship that runs hot and cold. If you walk away now . . . I won't be waiting for you if you change your mind."

She laughed, the sound hitting him like a bucket of cold water. "I'm not asking you to wait for me, Bobby. This is *not* me suggesting a break. I'm saying that we're done. We've run our course. I spent the last decade loving you. *Ten years.* While you've loved someone else. I'm not going home only to wonder every day if she's back yet. If you're still waiting for her. And I'm not giving up my own life to move down here and hope you choose me." She hitched the strap of her bag over her shoulder. "I'm going home, and I'm finally going to move on. I'm going to *stop* loving you, once and for all."

Her fingers wrapped around the doorknob, and he once again pressed his palm to the door. His movements were gentle this time, however. His mind reeled.

She loved him.

Yet, she was going to walk away and then *quit* loving him?

"*Jewel*—"

A knock sounded on the other side of the door, and both of them jumped. Then finality settled over the room.

"That's my ride." She didn't look at him. "I have to go."

And he knew that he had to let her go. Time was up. He'd tried. And he'd failed.

Reluctantly, he lowered his hand. Taking a step back, he showed her that she was free to go. He wouldn't try to stop her. However, when she pulled the door open, it wasn't her car driver waiting on the other side of it. It was Bria.

Jewel's gaze whipped back to him, and he saw the crack.

The stoicism she'd been holding on to since walking out of his bathroom had fled. She was broken inside.

"Jewel"—he shook his head—"don't. Let me call you next week. Let's—"

"He's all yours," she said to Bria. Then she walked out of his life.

CHAPTER EIGHT

The afternoon dragged as Jewel sat in her office. It had been a week since she'd walked away from Bobby, and a week that she'd been working every spare minute to find a solution to not losing the Double B.

She reached for the cup of pens sitting on her desk and moved them to the other side. Then she moved them back. She shifted the position of the single folder lying in the middle of the flat surface, picked up then set down the tiny bull Bobby had given her as a teen. Nerves had eaten a hole through her, and if Mrs. Brandon didn't hurry and make it down for their appointment, she feared she might throw up.

"Bulls are fed, boss. Settled in for the night." Leon popped his head through the doorway, then pulled up short when he got a good look at her. "You okay?" His eyes narrowed as he took in the room.

"I'm fine." She sat ramrod straight.

"Your desk . . ." He motioned to the nearly clean space in front of her. It was typically littered with paperwork. "Are you moving out?"

She hoped not. After leaving Missoula, she'd finally made up her mind and had decided that she *did* want to enact her plan. At least, she wanted to attempt to. "I have a meeting with Mrs. Brandon." She then let him in on a bit of reality. She looked Leon straight in the eyes. "To discuss the future of the Double B."

"*Oh.*"

The man was smart. He'd been around for several decades more than she, and he'd known when he'd hired on the year before that things might change. Mr. Brandon had just died, after all, and everything could be up in the air when such a huge change occurred. Of course, given the way the past year had gone, neither of them had expected *any* changes.

"You'll let me know if I need to start looking for another job?" His tone went solemn.

She nodded. "We'll talk the minute I finish with the meeting."

Without further words, Leon retreated. They'd returned from that week's rodeo a couple of hours ago, and making excuses, she'd headed to her office and left Leon to handle the bulls. She suspected he'd just figured out why. But she'd needed time alone to prepare. To review her pitch. This wasn't going to be an easy sell.

"She's in the office." She heard Leon speak from outside the barn, and she pulled in a deep breath and rose to her feet.

Bobby's mother appeared a few seconds later, for once not in her usual scrubs, and when she offered a genuine smile, Jewel relaxed for the first time that day. Beth Brandon had always been good to her. Just as her husband had been.

"Please, have a seat," Jewel requested. But as the older woman moved into the room, her footsteps stalled.

Her gaze trained on something behind Jewel.

Jewel didn't have to glance behind her to understand. It was the gift she'd found waiting for her the weekend before.

"That's you." Astonishment filled Mrs. Brandon's features. "That's *phenomenal*."

When Jewel had returned to the office last Sunday, mentally drained from walking away from Bobby, she'd come face-to-face with a twelve-by-twelve-inch wooden placard of *her*. It was only one side of her face, her profile rising up out of the wood. Bobby had sculpted both profile and placard from a single piece of mahogany, using stains and finely carved details to perfectly capture her expression when speaking with bulls. He'd mentioned how mesmerizing that look could be a few weeks before, and upon seeing it, she'd collapsed into tears.

"Who did that?" Beth asked.

Jewel didn't speak. She couldn't. But Beth had to know the answer.

Jewel waited, and Beth finally lowered to her seat. She dragged her gaze to Jewel's. "Not Bobby?" she whispered.

Jewel nodded.

"But how?"

Beth studied the sculpture again, and Jewel watched as pieces of the puzzle seemed to click into place. Beth turned in her seat, looking back over her shoulder as if seeing through the walls of the barn and across the pasture. Seeing the studio where Bobby spent so much of his time.

"I never knew," she finally whispered. "Does he have more like this up there?"

He had a cabinet full. But that wasn't Jewel's place to share. "You probably should ask him that yourself."

Bobby's mother nodded, and Jewel found herself wanting

to say more. Wanting to suggest she demand her son not give up this part of his life. Jewel knew he had plans, that he'd always seen himself being a solid "provider" by getting a job that would support a family. But his talent was so extraordinary. He couldn't just turn a blind eye to it.

She kept her thoughts tucked away, however. Because that, also, wasn't her place. If she and Bobby were still together . . . maybe. But he was probably already back with Bria.

With the thought she'd done her best to avoid all week now forefront in her mind, she bit down on the pain of her loss and nudged the folder across the top of the desk.

"I have an offer I'd like to discuss," she said. "Concerning the sale of the Double B."

She and Bobby's mother then got down to business as Jewel presented her idea. She was young; therefore, it hadn't occurred to her at first that she could buy such an established business. The reality was, she'd long planned to start her own company. It wasn't a dream she'd talked about much, but she'd been tucking away money since she'd first started working. Her hope had been to buy land and start from the ground up by the time she turned thirty. But life didn't always work out as planned, and she was nothing if not flexible.

"So, what I want to present are two options."

She opened the folder and spread two single sheets of paper out for Mrs. Brandon.

"One, would be for you to stay on as investors. As you can see, I've broken down what I can put down and the loan I'd be willing to take in that situation. As well as how your invest-ments would pay out, what would happen on down years, and so forth. I'd be full operator of the business, having to manage any staff losses on my own, while you and your family could sit back and simply receive dividends."

As the other woman looked over the sheet of numbers, Jewel tucked her hands into her lap and crossed her fingers. She'd never intended to take on such a large loan, and at her age, had assumed banks wouldn't be thrilled to hand over that kind of cash. But surprisingly, in the scenario where the Brandons stayed on as investors, banks *were* willing to talk to her. Her reputation, as well as that of the Double B preceded her, and she had several loan officers willing to take on that risk.

"Option two would be a straight-up buyout."

This was where things got dicey. It's where she would bring her father on as cosigner of an even larger loan. Her parents' retirement would be at stake, but their faith in her was solid. This was also the option she hoped would be given the most consideration.

"I'm aware that I may not equally compete with Easup's final offer," she went on, "but I *want* the Double B, Mrs. Brandon."

The other woman looked up.

"I want it because it was Mr. Brandon's. Because my own blood, sweat, and tears are in these bulls, as well as his. I would honor your husband's legacy, Mrs. Brandon. That I can promise you. So, I'm asking that you and your family consider my offer. If it's a no"—she nodded—"then I'll totally understand. This is a business, after all, and I understand how businesses work. But if it's a yes, then I would spend my life making your husband proud."

CHAPTER NINE

Cheers rose from the crowd as bull and rider shot from the chute. It was the last night of the competition, and Jewel stood on the sidelines fighting the urge to cry. This would likely be *her* last night as a part of the Double B, too. Mrs. Brandon hadn't announced the family's decision yet, but when Jewel made her pitch the week before, Bobby's mom *had* told her that Easup had already upped his offer. It came in slightly higher than hers, but the more important aspect of his offer was that if Rolls Royce remained unridden tonight, Easup would toss in a twenty percent bonus.

Who wouldn't take that?

And granted, it was possible that Rolls *wouldn't* pull it off. Nick Wilde had drawn Rolls, and Nick had been on fire lately. Which meant . . . she'd be rooting for Nick, whether that made her a bad stock contractor or not.

The rider went flying, and the crowd groaned.

"That was six point eight seconds, folks. Not quite enough to beat Urban Legend!" the announcer shouted.

After the bull fighters kept the animal from stomping on

the rider, the bull left through the gate, and Jewel's nerves inched higher. Four more before Nick and Rolls were up. They would be the last of the night.

However the evening ended, though, she *wouldn't* be looking for a new job tomorrow. She'd made that decision over the last couple of weeks, as well. She no longer wanted to work for another owner. She might be young, but she was good. And she knew it. If she didn't get the Double B, she was prepared to strike out on her own now. Not wait until she was thirty. Her parents were on board with that plan, as well, and were prepared to support her any way they could.

She caught sight of Leon farther down the railing and offered a tight smile. She'd left him to handle most everything this weekend, as she'd been a nervous wreck. He understood the gravity of the situation and was prepared to move on if he had to. But like her, he would prefer to stay with the Double B, as well.

The next bull charged from the gate, and the crowd rose to their feet. This rider was a top contender and stood an excellent chance of winning the weekend.

Eight seconds passed, the buzzer sounded, and the cowboy jumped free.

Jewel smiled and blew out the breath she'd been holding, her adrenaline pumping. She loved a good ride. She also really liked this guy. He was older than some of the others but hadn't yet lost his touch.

She glanced down the line of chutes and wiped her palms over the front of her jeans. Crawley was next.

Her heart hammered even harder. They were inching closer to Nick.

It took a couple of minutes for Crawley's form to emerge

from the huddle of riders, but his lanky body finally appeared, confidently climbing the rungs of the back gate. As he braced himself on either side of the bull, someone stepped to her side, but she didn't look over. She assumed it was either another rider or stock contractor, anxious to see how the night would end. However, when a hand she recognized rested on the top railing, her gaze darted to her right.

Blue eyes stared back at her.

"Bobby." She said his name as if he were the last person she'd expected to see tonight. And he was.

"You were right." He didn't bother with a greeting. "I can't give up carving. That's a part of who I am."

She sucked in a quick breath. Well, at least one good thing had come from their time together. "I'm glad to hear it. I think that's a healthy decision."

She turned back to the action instead of saying anything more, her nerves pinching even tighter. Her heart thundered. Why was he there? She didn't want to ask for fear the answer wouldn't be what she wanted to hear—she didn't *know* what she wanted to hear! And she also didn't want to risk reaching for him and admitting how much she'd missed him these past two weeks.

He hadn't called. Not that she'd expected him to. But she'd found that she *had* wanted him to.

She'd also wanted to tell him she'd been wrong. That she *would* wait for him. But she'd stuck to her guns, reminding herself that she wouldn't compete with Bria. She wouldn't be second choice.

"I also talked to Mom this week."

She flinched. *Crap*. Was that why he was there? Because his mom had seen the piece he'd made?

Crawley's gate flew open before she could come up with a reply, and the noise level precluded them being able to speak. She had eight seconds to gather her thoughts.

Eight seconds before she had to face him.

Bobby had clearly come to get something off his chest, so she'd let him do it. But she certainly hoped he wasn't about to lay into her for his mom seeing his gift. That hadn't been on her.

Once Crawley finished his ride—staying on for the full eight seconds—she took a moment to drag in a deep breath and lock down her emotions. She then turned to Bobby. There were two more riders before Nick. Hopefully, Bobby could say his piece and be on his way in that amount of time.

"I'm sorry if your mom seeing your gift upset you." She stared into eyes now burning with such intensity it almost set her back on her heels. She didn't let the look sway her, though. "I asked for a meeting, and she happened to see it in my office."

"That's fine. I wouldn't have given it to you if I hadn't wanted it to be seen."

"Then why are you here?"

She didn't take her eyes off him. What could have possibly been worth several hours of travel to seek her out?

And then a thought occurred. Had *he* been sent to tell her they were selling to Easup?

Her stomach dropped.

"The fact is," Bobby went on, not answering her question, "I should have showed my work to Mom before. To Dad, too. I should have shown them everything I've ever made."

She didn't disagree. "So, why didn't you?"

The vehemence in his gaze flickered for an instant, and his

Adam's apple moved as he swallowed. "I didn't because I wanted to make them proud."

His words made no sense, so she didn't reply. She waited.

He finally lifted his shoulders. "I know it might sound lame, but I've watched my parents support each other all my life. I wanted that kind of pride from them, as well."

"And what?" She still didn't get it. "Woodworking isn't something to be proud of?" With *his* skill?

His brows shot up. "A career in the arts, you mean?"

"Ah." The answer finally clicked. "The arts isn't exactly a guaranteed moneymaker, is it?" It wouldn't be the "provider" occupation he'd always envisioned himself holding. It wouldn't guarantee that he, alone, could take care of a wife and family.

"All I've ever wanted is someone to look at me the way they looked at each other."

"And let me guess." She crossed her arms over her chest. "Bria looks at you that way?"

Annoyance flickered over his face. "I'm not here to talk about Bria."

"Then I ask again . . . what *are* you here for?"

The crowd cheered, but she didn't look around. She didn't care how the rider did. She wanted to know what this conversation was actually about. And then she wanted to get on with her life, to find herself a piece of land and start her own company.

And she wanted to try to get over Bobby Brandon once and for all.

But then Bobby took her hand in his . . . and it felt so danged good.

"Jewel." The intensity was back. "I'm trying to pour my

heart out here. Would you please let go of that chip on your shoulder for one minute and listen?"

Tears threatened. That fast, and with one touch, and she was about to bawl like a baby. She loved this man too much, and she'd screwed up by walking away and not agreeing to keep trying. She wanted to tell him all of that. Tell him that she'd look for land near Missoula. She didn't have to work out of Birch Bay. She wanted to be with him. But did he still want to be with her?

"Jewel," he said again, and she realized she hadn't answered him.

She blinked to hold back the tears. "I'm listening. You have one rider left, and then we have to pay attention. Nick is riding Rolls tonight."

His lips curved at that, and she almost leaned into him.

"Mom came down last week and brought some of my pieces with her," he told her. "She also brought a whole heck of a lot of attitude. She couldn't believe I've never shown her any of that."

Jewel opened her mouth to add her two cents, but Bobby put a finger to her lips.

"I always thought following in Mom's footsteps would make them more proud. Doing *anything* with a solid career path. Dad had been the best, even before he started the Double B—and I couldn't ride a bull for anything—and Mom is top of her field. My brother and sister . . . they kill it in their careers. So *whittling* wood?" He shook his head. "But Mom had that look in her eyes when she came to see me. The one I'd thought she reserved only for Dad."

A tear escaped.

"She made me see that I've been living with a high school 'dream' that I never moved past."

His finger on her lips turned less pressing and more caressing.

"Bria and I came up with a plan years ago. And it was a good one. I thought it was what I wanted. But somewhere along the way, I lost sight of the real goal. A person's path should be about living. About finding who *they* are. What makes them happy. And *who* makes them happy."

"And Bria—"

"Stop." Anger fired through his eyes. "Don't you dare say her name again. You know she isn't who makes me happy. Are you just trying to piss me off? It's *you*, Jewel. You see *me*. You *get* me. And I get you too, dammit. Bria and I were done long before you and I ever got together, even if it took me until this week to realize just how long ago that was. We talked when she came over. We were both stuck in the past. Trying to fit a square peg into a round hole. So, don't say her name again. *You're* my person. You see me for who I am. You *love* me for who I am."

He finally quit talking, and she didn't know what to say. She just stood there in shock.

Noises filtered in from the crowd, but she couldn't pull her gaze from Bobby's. He slid his finger from where it remained over her lips and squeezed her hand in his. "Please tell me you still love me," he whispered. "That I'm not too late. I know you planned to come home and get over—"

"Stop." Her mind spun in circles. "Just stop. Of course, I still love you. Are you crazy? I've loved you my whole life. How could I stop in two weeks?"

A smiled cracked over his face.

"And I'll even wait for you, too," she hurried to say. She didn't want to hold anything back. And she wouldn't mess up this second chance. "We can do the long-distance thing. Or I'll move to Missoula. I'm going to start my own stock contracting company. I can do that from anywhere."

Confusion wrinkled his brow. "I don't want to do long distance. Are you not hearing what I'm telling you?"

She stopped talking. What had she'd missed?

"I'm moving back to Birch Bay, Jewel. Actually, I already have. That's why I was so late getting here. I quit school, and I moved all my things back home today. I'm going to sink or swim with my wood carving."

She blinked, unsure she'd heard correctly. And then she heard Nick's name being announced. *"Rolls is up!"*

She turned back to the arena just in time to see Nick give the nod. This was it. Either she lost the Double B right now, or an inkling of hope could remain.

The clock counted up, and Rolls bucked. But Nick held on.

Bobby slipped his hand down to clasp hers, and she gripped it as if she'd drown without his touch. And she just might. She loved this man. And though he had yet to say it, she was pretty sure he loved her, too.

At seven point nine seconds Nick lost his grip, and she groaned right along with the crowd. Her shoulders hunched forward. The bonus had just kicked in.

"There was one other thing I came here to tell you, Jewel."

She looked over at Bobby, the impact of her loss grounding her. Everything but Bobby blurred. Movement in her peripheral vision seemed to shift into slow motion.

"We can't go with either of your options," Bobby said, and she nodded robotically. She got it. She'd lost the Double B.

"I know," she forced out. "You're selling to Easup. You just made a lot of money."

"No. We're *not* selling to Easup." Bobby didn't look away, and she scrunched her eyes as her brain tried to catch up with his words. He wasn't making sense. "But we *did* create an option three," he told her.

The words took a minute to sink in. But when they did, a flicker of hope flared deep. She stood a little taller. "An option three?"

Was their option three something that would allow her to remain a part of the Double B?

She held her breath. "What is it?" she whispered.

Reaching for her other hand, Bobby turned her so that she faced him head on. And the most joyful look shone back at her. "Mom is splitting her portion of the business between us kids. Three ways. But neither Brady nor Brooklyn want to stay in, Jewel. They want to sell to you."

She replayed the words to make sure she'd heard them correctly, and then her heart rate sped up. "They do?" She bit her lip in anticipation.

"Yes. But I'm keeping *my* third." Bobby's eyes grew serious. "I'm not ready to give up Dad's legacy. That said . . . I'm hoping that if I'm a silent partner, you'll still consider buying us out. Two-thirds for you, one for me. You'll have complete control."

Fireworks exploding inside her couldn't have been more shocking. She couldn't believe what she'd just heard.

"It's really mine?" she said.

"It's *two-thirds* yours. If you want it. But it does come with one stipulation."

She nodded. She could handle whatever stipulation they

might have, because doing so would mean she got to keep Rolls and Death. And all the other bulls she'd been a part of. It would mean that she wouldn't have to start all over.

Staring up at him, almost too excited to form words, she asked, "What's the stipulation?"

"That you let me love you."

Her heart squeezed at the words. And then the most amazing feeling of warmth spread through her.

"That's all I ask," Bobby went on. "That you let me love you. I'm going to work on my art, live in Mom's apartment until I can talk you into getting a place with me"—he squeezed her hands tight—"and I'm going to love you for as long as you'll let me, Jewel."

Her tears returned. "You really do love me?"

"Baby." He wiped the moisture away with his thumbs. "I love you with every beat of my heart. How do you not know that already? And I'm going to *keep* loving you for the rest of my life."

EPILOGUE

It was the Montana Pro Rodeo Circuit Finals. A cold, snowy January day in Great Falls, Montana. But Jewel was warm inside the arena and having the time of her life. Bobby had convinced her to sit in the crowd this weekend, something she hadn't done in years, while Leon, Angi, and Daniel had all come along to handle the bulls.

"I'm glad you talked me into this," she told the man she loved. The man she'd not been a day without since he'd swooped in and turned her life upside down over four months before.

As Bobby had laid out, the Double B was now two-thirds hers. *And* Bobby was hers. And that was the best part. They'd moved in together almost immediately, and since he continued to work in the studio above his mother's garage, they saw each other anytime they wanted to. It was the perfect relationship. Jewel couldn't be any happier.

"I'm glad you let me talk you into it," Bobby murmured as he leaned into her side.

She bit her lip at his murmured words and at the way his

fingers skimmed over the top of her thigh. She knew he was thinking exactly what she was. They would be staying an extra few nights in Great Falls, sending the stock back with the others, and she couldn't wait to have this last day of the competition behind her so she could have her man all to herself. They'd both worked hard the last few months, and they deserved this time away.

"Last chance to lay bets on whether Rolls goes the distance," Bobby said. He'd been taunting her to bet with him on their own bull all weekend.

"No need to bet. You don't want me taking your money."

He chuckled. "The problem is we'd both be betting the same."

"That's true." They'd both bet on Rolls Royce. She might have wanted Nick to remain on their prized bull a few months ago, but that situation would be no more. Tonight she had every hope in the world that Rolls would remain unridden.

"JJ is ready." Bobby nodded toward the cowboy who currently straddled Urban Legend. JJ Parker had won the first round, with Crawley pulling ahead in the second. Nick had been only a fraction of a point behind both times. Any of the three could still take the weekend—as well as year-end winner. They were down to the last three rides.

"Send bad vibes his way," she muttered. "I want Nick to win."

"Hmpf," Bobby harrumphed. "I'm still not certain Nick Wilde doesn't have the hots for you."

"What?"

The gate was opened before either of them had time to say anything more, and leaning forward, they both gripped the railing and watched as man and animal leaped forward. JJ was putting in a good ride, but Urban Legend showed off, as well. Both athletes fought hard for the win, and after what seemed twice as long as reality, the buzzer sounded. JJ had made it the full eight seconds. He bound to the ground, and the bull-fighters jumped into action.

"That was a nice ride," Bobby declared. "It might win him the night."

"It might, but Nick could still come out on top." Crawley had drawn Rolls Royce, so being the good owner that she was, she gave little credence to the final man staying on. And then she recalled what Bobby had said just before JJ's ride. She turned his way. "Why would you think Nick has the hots for me?"

"Oh." A hint of pink touched his cheeks. "I was just teasing."

She didn't think so. She jabbed him in the ribs. *"Why?"*

Before he could answer, the rodeo clown took control of the mic. He turned everyone's attention to him and the announcer with a skit about catching rainwater in a bucket. But given that both Jewel and Bobby had seen that skit numerous times, she refocused on Bobby.

"Why?" she pressed.

He lifted her hand and kissed her fingertips. "I *am* kidding." His eyes twinkled with mischief as he kept her fingers pressed to his lips. "But I *was* jealous of the guy."

She shook her head. *"When?"* He knew she and Nick had been friends for years.

"At the cherry festival last year."

"At the . . ." She paused, thinking back to that time. That's when she'd cockblocked *him* with Ashlee Anderson. When *she'd* been so jealous she could barely see straight. And right before doing that, when she'd thought Bobby had eyes only for Ashlee and her expansive cleavage, she'd been standing on the other side of the road talking with Nick. She grinned. She learned something new about their relationship every day. "So, it wasn't just me who was jealous that day?"

Bobby shook his head, and Jewel could see by the way his eyes darkened that he was ready for the day's competition to be over. "It wasn't just you, babe. Lightning struck that day."

"I'm glad it did."

He nodded. "Me, too."

And, like him, she would also be glad when the weekend's events were over. She suddenly didn't care so much whether Nick *or* Rolls Royce took top honors.

She leaned in. "Bobby—"

"I have one more thing to show you guys and gals this afternoon," the rodeo clown announced, the volume of his voice seeping into the lovefest already in play in Jewel's mind.

She sat up straighter when she realized the entertainer had made his way near where they sat in the front row. He stopped on the other side of the railing.

"This one needs a volunteer," he declared, scanning his gaze back and forth as he searched the crowd both high and low. But then he zeroed in on her. "How about you, pretty lady?"

She snorted, but the crowd loved it.

"It'll just take a minute, darlin'." The clown winked, and she rolled her eyes. She'd known the guy for years and wouldn't put anything past him. There was no telling what he was up to, but she would go along with it.

"What do you need me to do?" she asked, and his grin went wicked.

"I simply need you to stand up."

She stood, and he cocked his head to the left. Then the right.

His hand went to his jaw in contemplation. "No." He shook his head. "That isn't quite right."

She looked down at herself. "Well, this is what you've got to work with. Take me or leave me."

Again, with his wicked smile. "I'll take you."

She glanced at Bobby, a smile on her face, but Bobby had his gaze on the other man instead of her. He didn't seem annoyed with the teasing flirtation, but not entertained, either. Just . . . focused.

"I'll take you," the rodeo clown said again, "but I *am* going to need you to climb right up here." He patted the top of the railing. "Just prop your tushy right down here, little miss."

She chuckled but did as she was asked.

Once in place, with both feet dangling over the inside of the railing, the rodeo clown studied her again. Head to the left. Head to the right. Hand to the jaw. He pursed his lips and looked her up and down, and the back of her neck began to itch as the entire crowd went quiet.

What could they all sense that she had yet figure out?

"I've got it!" he announced, holding one hand up high in the air. "I need you to spin, right where you are." He dipped one finger into a downward motion and circled it in the air. "Face the opposite direction, please."

She was beginning to have doubts about this whole skit, but still . . . did as she'd been asked. And that's when she saw Bobby.

Her breath caught. Bobby was on one knee . . . in front of her—and the entire crowd—with a ring box in his hand.

Jewel gulped.

Someone handed Bobby a microphone, and the few remaining voices went silent.

"Jewel Jackson," Bobby began. "Montana's own, Montana's *favorite* stock contractor—"

A whoop went up in the crowd.

He grinned inside his full beard. "You make me a better man, Jewel."

The crowd once again silenced.

"You bring out the *me* I always dreamed of being. You never cease to amaze me with who *you* are, and you have this way of looking at me . . ."

She looked at him exactly that way right then. The way she knew his parents had always looked at each other.

"I can't imagine living any part of the remainder of my years without you, sweetheart. Nor can I think of any place more suited to declare my everlasting love."

She grinned. She'd had no idea her man could be such a showman.

"I love you, Jewel Jackson. With my entire heart. Will you do me the honor of marrying me?" He opened the small box to display a *huge* ring. "Of letting me be your man for good?" He rose to his feet and pulled the microphone closer, and his voice went even deeper. "And of never *ever* bucking me off?"

She snorted with his last words, but the sound was mixed in with tears.

Happy tears.

He was so darned sweet.

"I don't think I heard an answer, did y'all?" the rodeo clown asked the crowd.

They screamed in agreement, and he put a microphone to Jewel's mouth.

"What do you say, Jewel?" It was Bobby speaking again. "You and me forever?"

She looked around the arena. She couldn't believe Bobby was proposing to her this way. But then again, this was her life. *Their* life. And she wouldn't have it any other way. "I can agree with that," she hedged, "but my agreement *does* come with one stipulation."

Bobby smiled. He got her reference. He'd added a stipulation to her buying two-thirds of the Double B.

"Anything you want." This time it was he who looked at her with unending love.

"I want you to let me love *you. Forever.*"

She was pretty sure he said "Done," but the crowd went wild, drowning out any words he might have uttered, and Bobby wrapped her tight in his arms. She'd loved this man for so long. She never imagined this would be her life.

But there was one thing that could make this night even more magical.

As Bobby slipped the ring on her finger, the announcer took over. "Enough of the romantic shenanigans, folks. We have a rodeo to finish. Two rides to go, and one winner to announce. Who will it be, ladies and gentlemen? Let's get this show on the road and find out!"

She and Bobby kissed as they lowered back to their seats, and as everyone quieted once again, Nick Wilde rose up over his bull. It was one of Adrien Easup's stock. The same bull James Crawley had *not* stayed on the night Bobby first announced his undying love.

"He's got to score big," she murmured.

"He will."

Bobby took her hand.

Neither pulled their eyes from the chute until the gate was opened. Then they didn't take their gazes off Nick. The bull kicked high, legs extended fully. He spun hard, he bucked. He kicked and fought. But through it all, Nick stayed on. With his own body extended in perfect form, it was an excellent ride. Probably the best she'd seen from Nick that year.

Eight seconds later . . . and the rider sat strong. The score would be good. And the arena went wild.

Nick's grin could be seen by every spectator in the place, and Jewel noticed that more than one of the famed buckle bunnies had eyes on the man currently in center ring. Nick wouldn't go to bed lonely that night, that was for sure.

The cheers died back down more quickly than usual as all eyes waited for the score. JJ's had been a 94, so Nick had to beat that number for this round. And a 95 would land him not only best for the weekend but best for the year. Assuming, of course, that Crawley didn't follow up with a better ride on Rolls.

"That's a ninety-five point one, folks!"

Bobby slung an arm around Jewel.

"I think he's going to do it," she said. If Nick pulled it off, this would be his first year to win top honors, but she doubted it would be his last. He was already good enough to go pro.

"Finishing the day is James Crawley on the newly engaged Double B Pro Rodeo's own, Rolls Royce."

Jewel grabbed Bobby's hand where it hung down over her shoulder and held on tight. This was it. Either this would be her first year solo with an unridden bull . . . or she would go home with *only* a brand-new sparkler on her left finger.

She glanced down at the emerald-cut diamond. She loved Bobby more than words could say.

"I love you," Bobby whispered in her ear.

She smiled over at him, and he captured her lips with his.

"And I love you," she mouthed back after they separated. And then Crawley and Rolls broke free.

She and Bobby sat immobile. Neither of them breathed for the next few seconds, and their only movements were their gazes shifting from rider to the clock.

Four.

Five.

Six.

Seven . . .

Crawley went off at seven point eight, and Bobby scooped Jewel up in his arms.

"You did it, babe!" He kissed her long and hard in the middle of the screaming crowd, and though Jewel had the thought that she never wanted to let go, it was she who pulled back. But she did so only to clasp Bobby's face in her hands. Her life was so much more than she'd ever imagined. And there was so much still that she wanted to experience with this man.

"*We* did it," she corrected. "It's you and me, Bobby. It'll always be *you and me*."

He nodded in agreement. "I couldn't love you more."

ABOUT THE AUTHOR

Photography by Amelia Moore

As a child, Kim Law cultivated a love for chocolate, anything purple, and creative writing. She penned her debut work, "The Gigantic Talking Raisin," in the sixth grade and got hooked on the delights of creating stories. Before settling into the writing life, however, she earned a college degree in mathematics, then worked as a computer programmer while raising her son. Now she's pursuing her lifelong dream of writing romance novels—none of which include talking raisins.

A native of Kentucky, Kim now resides in Middle Tennessee. You can visit Kim at www.KimLaw.com.

facebook.com/kimlawauthor

instagram.com/kimlawauthor

twitter.com/kim_law

amazon.com/author/kimlaw

bookbub.com/authors/kim-law

goodreads.com/kimlaw

DON'T MISS ALL THE WILDE BOOKS!

Sometimes the Wildes' cherry farm can feel like more of a burden than a blessing, but it proves to be the glue that holds the six siblings together in the wake of their mother's death. It is here that they learn to heal and grow, with all of them finding love while working through their own personal struggles. The Wildes of Birch Bay is a sweeping series about love, family, and what it truly means to return home again. Come along as compelling couples overcome conflict and challenges with courage, humor, and off-the-charts chemistry.

The Wildes of Birch Bay

Montana Inspired (prequel)

Montana Cherries

Montana Rescue

Montana Mornings

Montana Mistletoe (bonus story)

Montana Dreams

Montana Promises

Montana Homecoming

Montana Ever After (bonus story)

Made in the USA
Columbia, SC
10 November 2021